Dear Parent:
Your child's love of reading starts here!

Every child learns to read in a different way and at his or her own speed. Some go back and forth between reading levels and read favorite books again and again. Others read through each level in order. You can help your young reader improve and become more confident by encouraging his or her own interests and abilities. From books your child reads with you to the first books he or she reads alone, there are I Can Read Books for every stage of reading:

SHARED READING
Basic language, word repetition, and whimsical illustrations, ideal for sharing with your emergent reader

BEGINNING READING
Short sentences, familiar words, and simple concepts for children eager to read on their own

READING WITH HELP
Engaging stories, longer sentences, and language play for developing readers

READING ALONE
Complex plots, challenging vocabulary, and high-interest topics for the independent reader

ADVANCED READING
Short paragraphs, chapters, and exciting themes for the perfect bridge to chapter books

I Can Read Books have introduced children to the joy of reading since 1957. Featuring award-winning authors and illustrators and a fabulous cast of beloved characters, I Can Read Books set the standard for beginning readers.

A lifetime of discovery begins with the magical words **"I Can Read!"**

Visit www.icanread.com for information
on enriching your child's reading experience.

I Can Read Book® is a trademark of HarperCollins Publishers.

Spider-Man Versus the Lizard © 2010 Marvel Entertainment, Inc., and its subsidiaries. MARVEL, all related characters and the distinctive likenesses thereof: ™ & © 2010 Marvel Entertainment, Inc., and its subsidiaries. Licensed by Marvel Characters B.V. www.marvel.com. All rights reserved. Printed in the United States of America. No part of this book may be used or reproduced in any manner whatsoever without written permission except in the case of brief quotations embodied in critical articles and reviews. For information address HarperCollins Children's Books, a division of HarperCollins Publishers, 10 East 53rd Street, New York, NY 10022. www.icanread.com

Library of Congress catalog card number: 2009927734
ISBN 978-0-06-162620-3
Typography by John Sazaklis

09 10 11 12 13   LP/WOR   10 9 8 7 6 5 4 3 2   ❖   First Edition

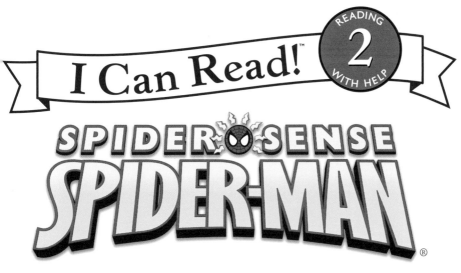

Spider-Man Versus the Lizard

by Susan Hill

pictures by MADA Design, Inc.

HARPER

An Imprint of HarperCollinsPublishers

PETER PARKER

Peter is a regular kid,
with a big secret:
He is also Spider-Man!

MR. JAMESON

Mr. Jameson is Peter's boss.
He wants Peter to take
pictures for his newspaper.

MRS. CONNORS

Mrs. Connors needs
Spider-Man's help.

THE LIZARD

Mrs. Connors's husband has
had a terrible accident.
He has turned into the Lizard!

SPIDER-MAN

Can Spider-Man find a cure for
the Lizard before it's too late?

"Welcome to Florida, Parker," Mr. Jameson said.

"Now, get to work!"

"Yes, sir!" said Peter Parker.

"But what is the story?" he asked.

Mr. Jameson wrote on a pad.

"Here's the headline," he said.

Peter read it.

"Monster Lizard Loose in Swamp!"

Peter took his camera to the swamp.

"It's quiet," he said.

Suddenly, Peter heard

a terrible roar.

He leaped into action!

"I may be a skinny kid
on the outside," Peter said
as he put on his mask.
"But I'm also Spider-Man!"

Spider-Man swung toward the
sound of the roar.

Then he saw something horrible,
big, and green.

"Gee, how did a little lizard
grow up to be a big, green monster
like you?" said Spider-Man.
"And what's with the lab coat?"

The monster roared at Spider-Man.
"I used to be Dr. Curtis Connors,
until I drank this potion.
Now I am the Lizard!"

The Lizard lashed his tail

and knocked Spider-Man down.

"Hey, watch that thing!"

said Spider-Man.

"I am making a giant lizard army,"
said the Lizard.

"I will rule the world!"

"That's a slimy thing to do,"
said Spider-Man.

The Lizard picked up
Spider-Man in his powerful claws
and threw him into the air.

Spider-Man landed in a tree.

"Talk about a crash landing,"

Spider-Man said.

There were big, hungry crocodiles

under the tree.

"Time to floss!" said Spidey.

Spider-Man shot out strong webs

and shut the crocodiles' jaws.

Then Spider-Man saw a house.

The name on the mailbox
was Connors.

Spidey swung down on a web
and knocked on the door.

A woman answered.

She was crying.

She told Spider-Man she was

the wife of Dr. Connors.

"Underneath that lizard skin, he is still my husband," she said. "He is Dr. Connors and the Lizard, in the same body!"

"Dr. Connors is just like me!"

thought Spider-Man.

"I'm a kid and a Super Hero,

in the same body!"

Mrs. Connors showed Spider-Man
her husband's lab.

"This is where he made a potion
to regrow arms and legs
the way lizards can," she said.
"He wanted to help people.
But something went wrong!"

"Dr. Connors is a good man
trapped inside an evil monster
he can't control,"
said Spider-Man.
"I must find a cure!"
Hours later, the cure was ready.
"I've done it!" cried Spider-Man.
"The Lizard must drink it
before it's too late!"

Just then the Lizard came in.

"Perfect timing!" said Spider-Man.

Spidey tried to grab the monster.

But the Lizard slashed his claws

and snapped his jaws.

"That's a cold-blooded thing to do," said Spider-Man.

Spidey sprang away and shot a web. The Lizard broke it with one thrash of his powerful tail.

The Lizard opened his jaws to roar.

Spider-Man saw his chance.

He poured the cure

down the monster's throat!

The Lizard thrashed
and roared.
"I can't tell if it's working!"
cried Spider-Man.

But suddenly,

the Lizard's skin became flesh.

"I'm human again!" said the doctor.

"And I never got any pictures

for my story," Spidey said quietly.

"Thank you!" said Dr. Connors.

"It's good to be myself again!

It was hard to be

one thing on the outside

and another on the inside!"

"I know,"
said Spider-Man.
"Believe me, I know."